Young People's

Stories
of
Friendship

Friendship is...understanding what a friend really needs.

Friendship is...sharing thoughts, feelings, and belongings.

Friendship is...helping each other.

Friendship is...not turning your back on someone in trouble.

Friendship is...respecting each other's differences.

Compiled by
Henry and Melissa Billings

Young People's Press
San Diego

Editorial, design and production by
Book Production Systems, Inc.

Requests for permission to make copies of any part of the work
should be mailed to: Permissions, Young People's Press, Inc.
1731 Kettner Blvd., San Diego, California 92101.

Cover illustration by Len Ebert.

Published in the United States of America.

1 2 3 4 5 6 7 8 9 – 00 99 98 97 96
ISBN 1-885658-49-4

Young People's Stories of Friendship

1

A
Perfect Friendship

This story comes from Vietnam. As you read, think about what it takes to make "a perfect friendship."

Duong Le was a poor student. He had to work very hard to pay for his schooling. On the other hand, his friend Luu Binh was quite rich. Luu Binh could pay for school without working at all. One day Luu Binh learned that Duong Le's schoolwork was suffering because of the long hours he spent working. Luu Binh decided to help. He asked Duong Le to live with him until after their big test. Duong Le agreed. He moved in with Luu Binh, and the two friends began studying together.

Duong Le had no money. He knew he had to do well on the test if he wanted to improve his life. So he studied hard. Luu Binh was different. He had plenty of money. He didn't feel the need to study as hard. When the test finally came, Duong Le was well prepared. He passed easily. He got his degree and was appointed mandarin. Luu Binh, however, failed the test.

Luu Binh returned home feeling very sorry for himself. Soon after, he began to waste his fortune. The next year he took the test again. But again he was not well prepared and so again he failed.

By this time, he had wasted all his money. He thought of his old friend Duong Le, who had become an important government official. Perhaps he would help him. So Luu Binh swallowed his pride and went to ask Duong Le for help. Imagine his surprise when Duong Le refused to see him! Worse, Duong Le ordered his guards to drive Luu Binh away. Luu Binh trudged away, carrying all his possessions in a bundle at the end of a stick. His tired walk and sad face told the story of his failure.

That night Luu Binh arrived at a small roadside inn. He was greeted by the owner, a young woman named Chau Long. She welcomed him with a cup of steaming tea and

listened to the long story of his failures. Chau Long encouraged Luu Binh to try again. She suggested that he remain at the inn, and she promised to help him in every way possible.

Now, without any money, Luu Binh worked hard at his studies. The days passed quickly until at last the day of the big test arrived again. This time, when the results of the test were published, Luu Binh saw his name at the top of the list. He had passed! He could now become a mandarin like his old friend Duong Le. Luu Binh rushed back to the inn to tell Chau Long the good news. But she had disappeared. He searched for her everywhere, but he couldn't find her. At last he gave up, and left for his new job.

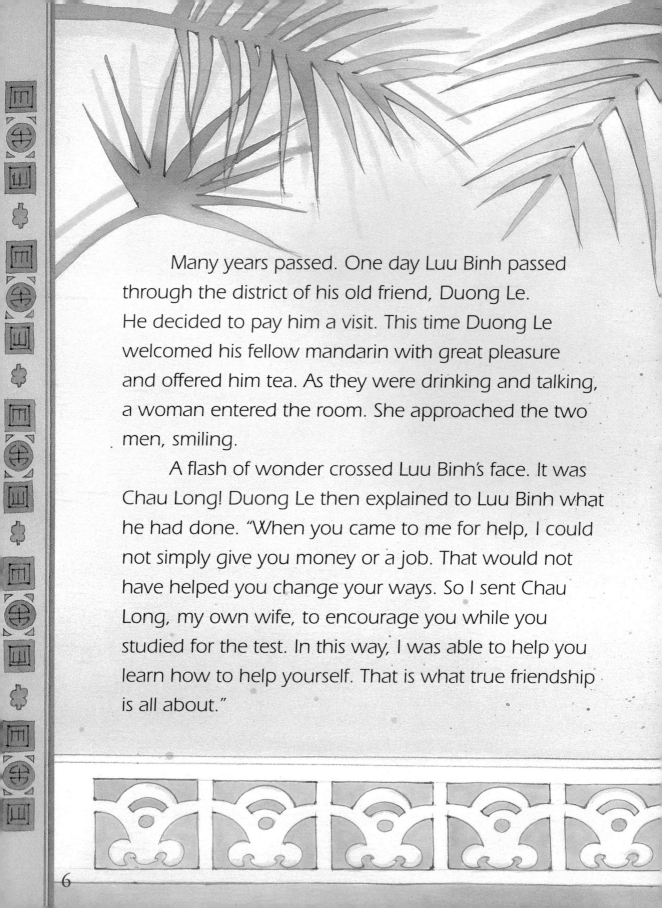

Many years passed. One day Luu Binh passed through the district of his old friend, Duong Le. He decided to pay him a visit. This time Duong Le welcomed his fellow mandarin with great pleasure and offered him tea. As they were drinking and talking, a woman entered the room. She approached the two men, smiling.

A flash of wonder crossed Luu Binh's face. It was Chau Long! Duong Le then explained to Luu Binh what he had done. "When you came to me for help, I could not simply give you money or a job. That would not have helped you change your ways. So I sent Chau Long, my own wife, to encourage you while you studied for the test. In this way, I was able to help you learn how to help yourself. That is what true friendship is all about."

Both men proved to be true friends. Luu Binh shared his home with Duong Le so the poor young man could study more. Later, when Luu Binh needed help, Duong Le responded in a way that seemed cruel at the time but was really in the best interest of his old friend. In this "perfect friendship," each friend found the way to help the other.

THE Lion's ADVICE

This story comes from the Ashanti people of Ghana. When two friends face a common danger, should they help each other?

There were once two friends, Kwasi and Kwaku. One day they went to the woods. They had been playing there for some time when they saw a lion coming. Right away, Kwasi climbed the nearest tree. Kwaku tried to follow him, but he couldn't climb very well. He had to give up.

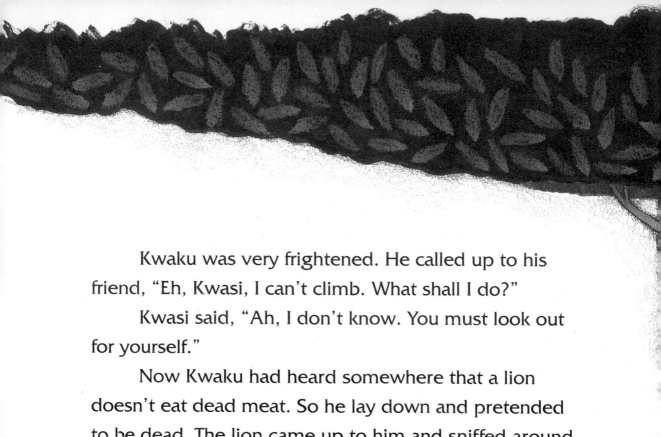

Kwaku was very frightened. He called up to his friend, "Eh, Kwasi, I can't climb. What shall I do?"

Kwasi said, "Ah, I don't know. You must look out for yourself."

Now Kwaku had heard somewhere that a lion doesn't eat dead meat. So he lay down and pretended to be dead. The lion came up to him and sniffed around for a while. Then the lion walked off.

Kwasi came down from the tree and said to Kwaku, "Oh, Kwaku, I thought you were dead. What was the lion saying to you just now?"

Kwaku told Kwasi, "Well, Kwasi, he said a lot of things to me. The most important one was that I should choose my friends better. So when we leave here, you and I will part company for good."

Kwasi was not a very good friend. He made no effort to help Kwaku. The lion gave Kwaku good advice. He told Kwaku to find friends who will help when you are in danger.

THE THREE FRIENDS

This story comes from Burma. As you read the story, think about the ways good friends can help each other in times of danger.

Once upon a time there were three animals who lived by the shores of a lake. They were close and loving friends. One was a Crow, the second was a Turtle, and the third was a Deer.

Now it so happened that a hunter passed
by the lake one day. He saw the Deer's hoof-
marks in the ground. The hunter laid down a
net in order to ensnare the Deer. Then he
went home, planning to return at daybreak to
see if the Deer had been caught.

As evening approached the Deer came
running back toward the lake to meet his
friends as usual. Suddenly he found himself
trapped in the hunter's net.

The Crow was the first to get back to the lake, and she waited alone there for some time. It wasn't at all unusual for the Turtle to be late, but the Crow felt worried about the Deer. So she flew off to search for him. In a very short time she found him caught in the net.

"Don't worry, friend Deer!" she called out. "Turtle and I will get you free. Just be patient for a while!" And the Crow flew off to find the Turtle.

The Crow soon caught sight of the Turtle, plodding his way slowly toward the lake.

"Hi, friend Turtle!" called the Crow. "Deer is caught in a hunter's net. Come with me and let us try to free him!"

So the Crow and the Turtle hurried along to the place where the Deer was caught in the net. The Turtle gnawed away at the cords while the Crow brought water in her beak to help soften the cords. All night they toiled away, but still they had not made a hole big enough to allow the Deer to escape. Dawn was coming. The hunter would return soon. The friends decided that the Turtle should continue to gnaw at the cords. Meanwhile, the Crow should fly to the top of a tree to keep watch.

No sooner had the Crow perched on the treetop than she saw the hunter marching along toward the lake.

"Quick, Turtle, quick!" called the Crow. "The hunter is coming!"

"Oh, I haven't half finished yet," the Turtle called back in despair. "What shall we do?"

The Deer became wild with fear. He began to leap and struggle. The hard work which the Turtle and the Crow had done during the night had greatly weakened the net. There was a ripping sound, and snap! the Deer broke free! He galloped as fast as he could away from the lake. The Crow followed, flying high above the trees.

Turtle too set off. But he could not move rapidly like the Deer, nor could he go up high like

17

the Crow. So when the hunter arrived at the net, he found the Deer gone, but he saw poor old Turtle plodding away nearby. So he stooped down, picked up the Turtle, popped him in his hunter's bag, and continued on his way.

"Oh, dear," thought the Crow, who was looking down from above, "poor old Turtle. We shall have to rescue him now!"

So the Crow flew off to find the Deer. When she had caught up with him she said, "Friend Deer! Now you are free, but the hunter has caught friend Turtle and put him in his bag."

"We must help him," said the Deer at once. "But how are we to do it?"

"I have an idea," said the Crow. "Go back to the path the hunter is following. Then, when you are in sight of him, pretend you are lame."

The Deer did so at once. When the hunter saw the Deer limping along the path ahead of him, his face lit up.

"Aha!" he cried. "So you hurt your leg, did you, when you were getting out of the net? Well, you are not going to get away from me a second time." With that, he put down the bag he had been carrying and took off after the Deer.

The Crow flew low over the Deer and whispered to him, "Now, lead him into the thick of the forest and then come quickly back here!"

The Deer limped on, staying always a little ahead of the hunter, who hurried after him. On, on they went. The forest thickened and it became more and more difficult for the hunter to keep the Deer in view. At last the Deer was sure that the hunter was lost. He stopped limping and began to run, quickly disappearing from the hunter's sight. He ran to the edge of the forest and back to where the hunter had left his bag. Crow was there.

The Deer hooked one of his horns into the flap of the hunter's bag and opened it with one flick. Friend Turtle came creeping out.

Then, before the hunter had time to find his way back to the spot, the three animals started off for a safe place in the forest.

The three good friends had escaped from the hunter and were together again.

Crow, Turtle and Deer were close friends. When Deer got into trouble, Crow and Turtle did every-thing possible to help him. When Turtle got caught, Deer returned the favor even though he was fright-ened. Friends are like that. They always try to help each other.

THE DIAMOND IS YOURS

This story comes from Mexico. Read to find out how an old man decides which of his three sons is the most worthy.

Once there was a very old man who was about to die. He wanted to leave a diamond, the only wealth he had, to one of his three sons. But he could not decide which one.

23

He called the three sons into his room, and this is what he told them: "My sons, I am not a rich man. The only thing I have that is worth much is this diamond. It has been in our family for generations, and I would not want it sold. Because it cannot be sold or divided, I can give it to only one of you. The diamond will go to whichever of you does the most noble deed in a week's time. Go now. Return in a week to tell me what you have done."

A week passed, and the sons returned. They found their father even weaker than before and unable to leave his bed. He asked each in turn to tell his story.

"My father," said the first son, "I thought and thought of a deed that would be worthy. Finally, this is what I did. I gathered together all my property, divided it in half, and gave one half to the poor people of the city."

The old man shook his head. "Ah, that is a good deed," he said, "but not truly noble. After all, it is every man's duty to be as generous as he can to the poor."

"*Padrecito*," said the second son, "When I was returning home from work one day, I saw a little girl caught in the swift current of the river. Though I can hardly swim myself, I jumped into the river and pulled her out. The current was so swift, I almost drowned."

"That, too, is a good deed, and yet not noble," said the father. "Everyone should be willing to risk his or her life for the sake of a child."

Then the third son told his story.

25

"Father, a wonderful thing happened to me. I was walking high up in the mountains very early one morning. There I saw a man, wrapped tight in a blanket, sleeping at the very edge of a cliff! I could hardly believe my eyes. For if he turned this way or that, if he moved at all in his sleep, the man would be certain to fall over the cliff—thousands of feet to the valley below! I crept closer, as quietly as I could, for I didn't want to startle him. And guess who the man was? Sancho, my bitterest enemy!

"I moved as close to him as I could. Gently I put my arms around him. Suddenly his eyes opened and looked into mine. I saw he was afraid. 'Do not fear,' I said. I pulled him toward me and rolled with him, away from the cliff.

"We both stood up, and he said, '*Ay*! I came this way last night. It was so dark that I could not see my own feet! I was too tired to go on, so I stepped off the path to sleep. I had no idea where I was! I see now that if I had walked a little farther, or turned in my sleep, I would have become food for the vultures in the valley. You have saved my life, *amigo*!'

"We threw ourselves into each other's arms and swore to be friends forever. We wept for joy. Each of us found a friend, where before there had been an enemy!"

"Ah, my son!" exclaimed the old man. "That is a beautiful story, and a truly noble deed. It is a rare person who will risk his life to offer friendship to his enemy. The diamond is yours!"

Helping the poor and risking your life to save a child are both worthy deeds. But, as the old man said, they are also duties. People are expected to help the poor or save a child. But turning an enemy into a friend is quite different. It is not a duty. When someone does that, it is not only worthy but noble. That is why the third son earned the diamond.

Acknowledgments

Grateful acknowledgment is made for permission to reprint the following copyrighted material:

Adaptation of "A Perfect Friendship" from VIETNAMESE LEGENDS by George F. Schultz. Reprinted by permission of Charles E. Tuttle Co., Inc. of Tokyo, Japan.

Adaptation of "The Lion's Advice" from WEST AFRICAN FOLKTALES, translated by Jack Berry, 1991, p. 144. Reprinted with permission of Northwestern Press.

Adaptation of "The Three Friends" from BURMESE AND THAI FAIRY TALES by Eleanor Brockett. Copyright © 1965 by Eleanor Brockett. Follett Publishing Company, an imprint of Modern Curriculum Press, Simon & Schuster, Elementary. Used by permission.

"The Noblest Deed" adapted and retitled "The Diamond Is Yours!" from TALES THE PEOPLE TELL IN MEXICO by Grant Lyons. Copyright © 1972 by Grant Lyons. Julian Messner, an imprint of Silver Burdett Press, Simon & Schuster, Elementary. Used by permission.